GUINEA PIGS ONLINE CHRISTMAS QUEST

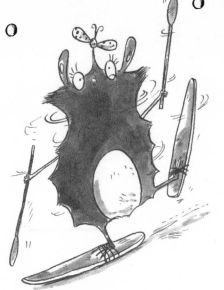

GUINEA PIGS ONLINE CHRISTMAS QUEST

Jennifer Gray
and Amanda Swift

Illustrated by
Sarah Horne

Quercus

New York • London

Quercus

New York • London

© 2013 by Jennifer Gray and Amanda Swift
Illustrations © 2013 by Sarah Horne

First published in the United States by Quercus in 2014

ISBN 978-1-62365-861-8

Library of Congress Control Number: 2014945595

Distributed in the United States and Canada by
Hachette Book Group
237 Park Avenue
New York, NY 10017

Manufactured in the United States

2 4 6 8 10 9 7 5 3 1

www.quercus.com

contents

1

the christmas cocoa bean

It was three days before Christmas and at number 7, Middleton Crescent, Strawberry Park, London, the preparations were in full swing.

The guinea pigs were decorating the hutch with holly and ivy they had brought in from the garden.

At least Fuzzy was decorating the hutch. Coco was lying on her back on a pile of soft straw dreaming about all the Christmas presents she was going to get from their owners, Ben and Henrietta.

"I want a new bow," she sighed. "And a bottle of bubble bath. And a purple hairbrush."

"You've got about five hairbrushes already," Fuzzy said. He finished weaving a piece of ivy around the water bottle. "Now come give me a hand with the tree." He grabbed a large piece of broccoli from their food bowl and started to heave it into the corner.

"I don't have a *purple* hairbrush," Coco complained. She rolled over and stared at the tree. Fuzzy had upended the broccoli onto its stalk. It sagged against the wire of the hutch.

Coco frowned. "It looks a bit lopsided," she said. "Can't you straighten it up?"

"Can't *you*?" Fuzzy chattered impatiently. He leaned against the broccoli tree, trying to prop it up. He couldn't wait for Christmas! A huge lunch of Brussels sprouts with gravy

followed by a whole afternoon lying
on Ben's lap watching adventure
films—it was Fuzzy's idea of heaven!
But first there was work to be done.

"Come on, Coco," he chattered
again. "Help me with the
decorations!"

"Definitely not!" Coco said. "One

never had to do things like that when one lived at Buckingham Palace."

Fuzzy made a face. Coco had once lived with the Queen, which was why she sometimes got all stuck up and talked in a funny way. It only seemed to happen when there was something she didn't want to do, like now.

Just then the door to the hutch flew open. A banana-colored guinea pig with a toffee-colored tummy scuttled in.

"Cooee!" It was Banoffee from next door. "I hope you don't mind, but we let ourselves in."

Although there was no longer a cat living at number 7, Middleton Crescent, Ben and Henrietta had kept the cat flap in the kitchen door. The guinea pigs used it as a door to the garden. And sometimes their friends used it to come see them.

Next came a skinny patchwork of fur with a wool hat.

"All right, guys?" It was Banoffee's oldest son, Terry.

After that there was a lot of squeaking as in tumbled thirteen little guinea pigs of different shapes and sizes. They were Banoffee's other children. And they all had lovely braids in their hair. Even the boys!

"They're very excited!" Banoffee shouted over the din. "They've just hung up their stockings, ready for Christmas!"

The door to the hutch swung open for a fourth time. A handsome black guinea pig with bushy eyebrows and silver speckles in his fur whizzed in on a scooter. He had a satchel around his neck. It was Eduardo, Coco and Fuzzy's friend who lived in the thicket at the bottom of the garden.

"I, Eduardo Julio Antonio del Monte, will tell the children a story about Christmas in my beloved homeland, Peru," he announced.

Eduardo was a type of guinea pig called an Agouti. He had been sent by his mother, the Queen of the Agoutis, all the way from Peru to free the guinea pigs of the world. But he'd gotten lost and ended up in Strawberry Park.

"I love stories!" squealed Blossom, the youngest of Banoffee's guinea piglets.

"Sit down, everyone," Coco said bossily. "In a circle." She couldn't

help being bossy in front of Eduardo.
Seeing him always made her want to
show off.

All the guinea pigs sat in a circle,
except Fuzzy, who was still holding up
the broccoli Christmas tree.

Eduardo waited for silence. Then
he began his story. "In my country,
there are many mountains and trees,"
he said. "There are lakes and rivers.
And even though in your winter it is
our summer, high in the mountains
where my family lives there is snow at
Christmas."

"I love snow!" Blossom whispered.

"Me too," Eduardo said. "Which is why I always carry ski poles in my satchel when I am in Peru."

Coco frowned. Now *Eduardo* was showing off. That was her job!

"Peru is a land of great beauty," Eduardo continued. "It is also a land of great danger for guinea pigs. Above the mountains flies a giant bird."

"Is it bigger than a pterodactyl?" asked Terry. "Only I've seen pictures of them on the Internet, and they're *enormous*."

"Bigger," Eduardo said, although he didn't know what a pterodactyl was. "It is the mighty condor. And man, does that bird like to eat guinea pigs!"

The little guinea piglets gasped at the thought of a giant guinea-pig-eating bird.

"It can't be worse than Renard," Coco said.

Renard was the fox who lived in the thicket. He was always trying to catch the guinea pigs, especially Coco.

"Pah!" Eduardo laughed. "The mighty condor makes Renard look like a squirl."

"A *squirrel*," Fuzzy said kindly, although his paws were aching from holding up the broccoli tree. "Not a *squirl*."

Eduardo shrugged. "It matters not, *amigo*, what you choose to call him.

What matters is that he has a beak like a pair of *skissors*."

Coco giggled.

Eduardo glared at her. "Only one guinea pig has ever been brave enough to take on the mighty condor," he continued.

"Who?" Blossom demanded breathlessly.

"Indiana Pig, our great guinea-pig hero," Eduardo explained. "He built a plane . . ."

"A plane!" repeated Fuzzy. He had always wanted to fly a plane.

"*Si*, señor, a plane. He flew up to

the top of the mountain to fight the condor so that guinea pigs could live without fear. But the condor was too strong for him."

"What happened?" asked Terry.

"The plane crashed," Eduardo told him. "Indiana Pig and his guide escaped. They hid in a secret cave in the mountains. Indiana Pig tried to return to the burrow, but there was a terrible storm and he became separated from his guide. Only the guide made it back home." Eduardo stifled a sob. "Indiana Pig was never seen again."

"Has anyone else tried to fight the condor?" Fuzzy asked.

"No, it is impossible," Eduardo said, "which is why each Christmas we Agoutis bring out our lucky charm. We believe it will keep us safe from the condor for another year."

"Oooh!" Coco's eyes lit up. "A lucky charm! What is it, a bracelet?"

"No, señorita, it is not a bracelet." Eduardo looked deadly serious. "It is our Christmas Cocoa Bean."

"Cocoa bean?" repeated Fuzzy.

"*Si*, señor," Eduardo nodded. "Instead of a tree at Christmas, it is

the tradition of
our family
to decorate
the lucky
Christmas
Cocoa Bean.
It must be on
the table when
we sit down to our

Christmas lunch of chickweed and
papaya juice. Or, Agouti legend says,
the mighty condor will eat us all up."

"What a lot of nonsense!" Coco said.

Banoffee's children stared at her,
wide-eyed.

"Excuse me?" Eduardo looked astonished.

"I said, what a lot of nonsense." Coco knew she was being horrible, but she couldn't stop herself. Sometimes, when Eduardo got all the attention, she felt mean words bubble up inside her and pop out of her mouth even though she didn't really want them to. "I've never heard anything so silly in my life."

A tear trickled down Eduardo's cheek. "Señorita," he sniffed, mounting his scooter, "you have hurt my feelings. I think I will go and sit in my lonely burrow and write a sad song to cheer myself up."

He scooted out of the hutch.

A moment later they heard the cat flap bang shut.

"We should probably go," Banoffee said. She and Terry gathered up the kids and shooed them out.

Fuzzy let the broccoli tree fall. "You shouldn't have said that, Coco," he said. "Don't you realize Eduardo must be missing his family? Christmas is a horrible time to be away from home."

"Oh, Fuzzy, I'm sorry." Coco

started to sob. "I didn't mean it."

Fuzzy passed her a scrap of newspaper to wipe her nose on.

"I know," he said. "The question is, what can we do to cheer Eduardo up?" He scratched the crest on his head. "We can't invite him for Christmas because Ben and Henrietta will notice."

Suddenly Coco's face brightened. She knew exactly what would cheer her up if she were sad. "I've got it!" she cried. "Let's get him a Christmas present!"

2
mummy!

Later on, when Coco left the hutch and crept out into the kitchen, she was very surprised at what she saw. It wasn't just that the dishes were done, although that *was* a surprise. (Ben and Henrietta always thought the other one would do the dishes.) It wasn't even that the Christmas cards were hanging around the room. (Ben and Henrietta always thought the other one was going to put them up.)

The fridge was talking. The door was open and the fridge seemed to be muttering to itself.

"That's so cool!" it said.

Coco stayed by the hutch. Either she or the fridge had gone mad. Then Coco heard Henrietta's sensible shoes clip-clopping down the stairs and coming into the kitchen. Coco scampered behind the sofa so she wouldn't be seen. She didn't want Henrietta to know she could get in and out of the hutch on her own.

"Mummy, come away from that fridge," said Henrietta firmly.

"But it's so lovely and cool, Henrietta."

Coco recognized the voice now.

Of course it wasn't the fridge talking. It was Mummy! Not *Coco's* mummy of course. It was Henrietta's mom, the Antarctic explorer. Everyone called her Mummy, even the guinea pigs, because that's what Henrietta called her. She always came to stay at Christmas, when she wasn't exploring.

"You know I've never gotten used to the hot temperatures here in England," complained Mummy.

"It's not hot here, Mummy. You're just used to Antarctica," said Henrietta. She shut the fridge door, to reveal a tiny old woman wearing a wool hat and a big puffy coat. "And you'd be a lot less hot if you weren't wearing all that gear."

"I need to dress warmly," said Mummy sulkily, "because I'm just about to go Christmas shopping."

Christmas shopping! Those two words were music to Coco's ears. This could be the perfect opportunity to get a present for Eduardo.

Coco raced across the kitchen. On the far side of the kitchen counter she saw Husky, Mummy's dog. He was munching a seal burger.

"Hi, Husky," said Coco, giving his paw a little hug.

Now you may think it very odd that she didn't scream and run away from Husky, because guinea pigs and dogs are not usually the best of friends. But Husky was specially trained not to harm other animals, because sometimes he had to help Mummy rescue them in Antarctica.

27

"Are you going too?" Coco asked.

"No. I do all my shopping on the Internet," Husky replied.

Up in the hall, Henrietta was saying good-bye to Mummy.

Coco pulled herself up the stairs, dashed over to Mummy's battered old handbag, and hopped in. Inside the bag it was dark and crunchy. That's because it was full of candy wrappers. There was also a brand-new cellphone. Mummy always had the latest technology.

Coco felt herself being lifted up. The front door banged. From inside

the bag she could just about follow
Mummy's route as she walked briskly
along Middleton Crescent and into
Upper Street. Then Mummy stopped.

Where were they? Coco peeped
out of the bag. Mummy had stopped
outside a shop. Coco read the sign—
FROSTY'S FROZEN FOODS. What on earth
was she going to get for Eduardo in
there?

Just then Mummy's cell rang. Coco
shrank back as Mummy's wrinkled
hand felt around in the handbag
and pulled the phone out. "Hello,
Dolores!" Coco heard her say.

Dolores was Mummy's best friend. Like Eduardo, she was from Peru, but unlike Eduardo, she still lived there. Coco wondered what she wanted.

She soon found out.

"You're going on an adventure?" Mummy screeched. "To find the lost gold of Magchu Pigchu?" Mummy gave a whoop of excitement. "What? Of course I'll come! I wouldn't miss it for the world. I'll be on the next plane to Peru!"

"Taxi!" Mummy hailed the nearest cab. "To the airport, as quick as you can!"

Coco rustled
around in the
handbag,
wondering
what to do.
A plane! To
Peru!

It was Eduardo who should be
going to Peru, not her! She felt all
wobbly inside. It was Christmas
in a couple of days. What if they
didn't get back in time for presents?
What if they didn't make it home for
Christmas lunch? What if she didn't
see Henrietta, or Ben, or Fuzzy on

Christmas Day? Suddenly Coco knew exactly how Eduardo must have been feeling away from his family.

The handbag opened. Mummy reached in, trying to find a piece of candy, but instead her hand found Coco. She pulled her out.

"Coco!" Mummy exclaimed. "How nice to see you. I hope you don't get motion sick." Mummy gave her a quick stroke, then popped Coco back into the bag and exchanged her for a toffee.

Coco felt like crying. She wanted to go home.

Just then the bag opened again

and Mummy's cellphone crunched onto the sweet wrappers beside her. The screen glowed.

Coco stared at it. Maybe she could contact Fuzzy and get him to alert Ben and Henrietta. Maybe Ben and Henrietta could pick her up at the airport before it was too late! Quickly she scrolled down Mummy's list of contacts. It was a pretty strange list, mostly of people who sold stuff for Antarctic expeditions. She got to H. Harold's Husky Hire, Harriet's Heated Hats . . . Phew! Henrietta was next on the list!

Coco hesitated. If Henrietta read a text message from Coco, she'd get a big shock! Henrietta and Ben didn't even know the guinea pigs could let themselves out of their hutch, let alone use a cellphone. She'd just have to hope Fuzzy saw it first.

> **Help!**

Coco texted.

> **I'm catching a plane to Peru with Mummy to find the lost gold of Magchu Pigchu. Coco xoxoxoxoxoxoxoxoxoxoxo.**

She pressed Send.

The screen went dark. Coco waited anxiously. After a few moments the screen lit up again. It was a message from Henrietta's phone.

Haha, we know! We're coming 2!
Mummy already txtd H & B. C u soon!
Fuzzy ☺

Coco felt a surge of relief. Fuzzy was coming! And Ben and Henrietta. They would all be together for Christmas. Then she remembered Eduardo.

> **What about E? C xoxoxoxoxoxoxoxoxo**

She waited for the reply.

> **Don't worry! He's hiding in Husky's pet carrier.** ☺

Coco couldn't help smiling in spite of everything. They'd all be together for Christmas after all.

And Eduardo would get to go back to his beloved homeland, Peru.

3
off to peru

Coco sat on Mummy's lap, her toes wrapped up in a cozy blanket. She was having a brilliant time. Dolores had bought Mummy a seat in first class. Coco gave a deep sigh of satisfaction. What more could a guinea pig ask for? The TV screen popped out of the arm of the seat! She had her very own headphones! A pretty lady in a hat had given her a lovely little velvet bag with guinea-pig-size bottles of shampoo and hair gel in it. In front of her was a tray of nibbles and a glass of fizzy carrot juice.

"Would you like a glass of champagne?" A handsome man in a smart blue jacket sat across the aisle from Mummy. He had a very sophisticated voice. Coco's heart fluttered. Then she realized he wasn't talking to her, he was talking to Mummy.

"Yes, please!" said Mummy.

"I'm Rupert de Vere," the man introduced himself. He ran his fingers through his thick hair. "I'm a mountaineer. I'm distantly related to the Queen."

"I'm Mummy," said Mummy. "I'm an Antarctic explorer. I'm distantly related to a snow monkey." She took a long drink of champagne and burped.

"Very pleased to meet you!" Rupert de Vere smiled. He had big teeth, the kind that a guinea pig would be proud of. "What takes you to Peru?"

Mummy looked around to make sure no one was listening. "The lost gold of Magchu Pigchu," she hissed. "A friend of mine's had a tip-off. There are some robbers out looking for it. We need to find it first and help the Peruvian people save it!"

Rupert de Vere shook his head sadly. "One can't trust anyone these days." He settled back down in his seat.

Coco felt her eyes closing. How lovely to meet someone who was related to the Queen. And who was classy, like her. She really hoped they'd bump into Rupert de Vere again, she thought as she fell into a deep sleep.

Two changes of plane later, they finally arrived at their destination.

"Why on earth are there giant sheep outside the airport?" asked Coco.

Outside airports in Britain there is usually a row of taxis, but outside the tiny mountain airport in Peru, there was a row of furry animals as well.

"They're not giant sheep, they're llamas!" said Fuzzy, who knew about them from the Internet.

The three guinea pigs peeped out of Ben's backpack.

"Holy guacamole!" Eduardo cried. "I don't believe it! This is near where my family lives!"

"Will we get to meet them?" asked Fuzzy excitedly.

"Maybe," Eduardo said. *"Hola, amigos!"* Eduardo greeted the llamas happily. "They will take us up into the mountains," he explained.

Just then an old woman, who was even tinier than Mummy and wearing an even bigger puffy coat, approached the group.

"Welcome, welcome!" She gave Mummy a big hug. "You must be Ben

43

and Henrietta! I'm Dolores. Delighted
you could join the adventure. Together
we will find the lost gold of Magchu
Pigchu before those rotten robbers
do!" Then she bent down and said
hello to the animals. Eduardo ducked
down inside Ben's backpack just in
time. None of the humans knew he

was there. In fact none of the humans knew he was anywhere, because they had never seen him.

"Come along! We need to get to the camp before nightfall," said Dolores. Ben helped her load the luggage onto the llamas' backs. The little group moved off, with Husky trotting alongside.

The guinea pigs could see massive snowy mountains in front of them. Eduardo began to sing softly:

"I'm Agouti, my beauty,
Los mountains are my home,

My peoples live in freedom,
Among the grass we roams."

"Shh!" Coco chattered at him. "The humans will hear you!"

"I am so happy to be home I cannot shush," Eduardo laughed. But he managed to hum quietly to himself as the procession made its way slowly along a track to the camp at the base of the mountains.

Dolores had booked a cabin for them.

"It's pretty basic," she said, opening the cabin door, "but I think you'll find it comfortable."

The cabin had two sets of bunk beds, a table and chairs, a tiny stove, and a sink. As she looked at the plain walls, Coco felt a little sad not to be in her cozy hutch in Strawberry Park, with its Christmas decorations. But she soon cheered up when Ben and Henrietta made a bed for the guinea pigs by the stove and gave them some food. Husky munched some dog biscuits and lay down beside them. Then, when all the humans had gone to sleep, Eduardo crept out of the backpack and snuggled up too.

"Muchos gracias, amigos," he said softly. "For this wonderful Christmas gift. Tomorrow you will meet my family."

"Wakey, wakey!"

Coco woke up and rubbed the sleep out of her eyes.

"Come!" It was Eduardo. "The humans have gone!"

Coco looked about. The cabin was empty. Husky and the humans must have gone up the mountain to look for the gold.

Then Coco realized that Eduardo
had disappeared too. All she could
hear were sounds of scratching and
banging.

"Where are you?"
Fuzzy demanded.

"Down here!"
Eduardo's voice
came from
somewhere under
the stove. "Hurry!
There is a secret
tunnel!"

Fuzzy and Coco
glanced at each other

nervously. The last time they'd been down a secret tunnel they'd almost been buried in mud! And, when they came out the other end, Renard the fox was waiting to eat them.

"No, thanks!" Coco shuddered.

"*Amigos,* I promise you, it is safe," Eduardo shouted. "My family uses it in the winter. When it becomes too cold in the burrow, they sneak into the cabins to warm up!"

"You mean there's a tunnel from every cabin to your home?" Fuzzy asked.

"Sure, *amigo,*" Eduardo's head

poked out from under the stove. "We Agoutis love to dig. Besides, that way the mighty condor can't catch us."

"All right then!" Coco was happy to be bossed around for once, because she was looking forward to meeting some Peruvian guinea pigs. And she didn't want to be eaten by the condor. She wriggled down the pipe after Eduardo. "Come on, Fuzzy!" she squeaked. "What are you waiting for?"

4
coco loco

A few minutes later the guinea
pigs emerged from the tunnel into
Eduardo's family burrow.

"Welcome to my home," Eduardo
said.

Fuzzy and Coco stared in
astonishment. All around them,

guinea pigs were putting the final touches to their Christmas preparations.

A warm fire glowed in the fireplace. Above it hung ten red-and-green wool stockings. Delicate snowflakes made out of white thread dangled from the ceiling like spiderwebs. In the middle of the burrow stood a low table made out of a plank of wood. The table was covered with a gold cloth and set with ten place mats woven from hay. Beside each mat was a tiny cup made from a nutshell and painted blue. In

the center of the table was a pile of green tinsel.

From somewhere beyond, in a part of the burrow Coco and Fuzzy couldn't see, a delicious smell of cooking wafted toward them.

"It's beautiful!" Coco breathed, gazing at the decorations.

"Delightful!" Fuzzy agreed, closing his eyes and sniffing the food.

"Thank you, *amigos*." Eduardo threw down his satchel. "Hey, everyone," he shouted. "I'm home!"

The Agouti guinea pigs turned in amazement.

"Eduardo?" A silver guinea pig with a gray nose emerged from the kitchen. She was a bit smaller than Eduardo, but had the same bushy eyebrows. Instead of a satchel she wore an apron and had a little crown on her head.

"Mama!" Eduardo yelled. He raced over and bowed, because even though she was his mom, she was still the Queen of the Agouti guinea pigs. Then he grabbed her around the middle, picked her up, and gave her a huge hug.

After that all the other guinea pigs crowded around, squeaking and squealing and hugging Eduardo and asking him questions in Spanish. Two baby ones who'd never even met Eduardo before, because they hadn't been born when he left, threw themselves on top of the heap of happy furry creatures and started squealing madly with excitement.

Eventually the squealing stopped. Eduardo shook off the babies and extended a paw toward Fuzzy and Coco. "Mama," he said, "I would like you to meet my good friends from London."

Fuzzy and Coco stepped forward. Fuzzy bowed. Coco curtsied. She wanted to show respect to the Queen of the Agoutis, but she also wanted it to be obvious that this was not the first time she had met a Queen.

"Bienvenido!" The Queen of the Agoutis smiled warmly. Then she clapped her paws and the Agouti guinea pigs scampered off in all directions.

"They have gone to prepare a welcome feast," Eduardo explained. "Come, *amigos,* let us sit by the fire and tell stories of olden times."

Coco and Fuzzy sat on cushions, munching chickweed.

Eduardo and his mum chattered away in Spanish. The babies tumbled around on the rug.

Suddenly there was a gust of wind. Another guinea pig blew into the burrow through the front door.

He looked very like Eduardo, except his fur was a deep copper color with silver speckles, instead of black. And strapped across his back was a guitar, not a satchel.

"Eduardo!" he cried in amazement.

"Bernardo!" Eduardo replied.

The two guinea pigs embraced.

Bernardo's eyes fell on Coco. "I am Bernardo Felipe Juan Carlos Jose Marino Ronaldo del Monte of Peru," he said smoothly. "Cousin of Eduardo."

Coco held out a paw. "I am Coco Loco del Posho of Buckingham Palace," she said, making up a fancy name because she wanted to impress him.

Eduardo frowned.

"And I'm Fuzzy," Fuzzy said.

Bernardo ignored him. "Coco?" he said quickly. "Your name is Coco—like our lucky Christmas Cocoa Bean?"

"So what?" Eduardo said rudely. "What's the big deal?"

"You mean your mother hasn't told you?" Bernardo said, astonished. He strummed a few chords on his guitar.

"Told me what?" Eduardo demanded.

The Queen of the Agoutis seemed to understand something was wrong, even though she didn't speak much English. She started speaking to Eduardo in a low, sad voice. Her eyes filled with tears. One of the babies had to go and fetch her a tissue.

When she finished there was a short silence.

"Caramba!" Eduardo looked shocked. "No way!"

"Yes way, Eduardo," Bernardo picked out a melancholy tune on his guitar strings. "It is bad, no?"

"What is?" Coco demanded.

"What's the matter?" Fuzzy asked.

Eduardo turned to his friends. "Remember, *amigos,* back in Strawberry Park, I told you about the Agouti legend of the lucky Christmas Cocoa Bean?"

Fuzzy nodded seriously. "Unless the lucky cocoa bean is on the table at Christmas, the guinea pigs will all be eaten by the mighty condor."

"Something terrible has happened," Eduardo whispered. "The lucky Christmas Cocoa Bean is gone!"

Fuzzy and Coco glanced toward

the table. The green tinsel in the center glittered brightly. But there was nothing on top of it.

"It has been stolen by the condor." Eduardo bowed his head. "Without the cocoa bean, the Agoutis are doomed."

Coco gave him a pat. "Don't worry about that old thing," she said. "I once had a lucky ribbon. I wore it every day for a month. Then Henrietta vacuumed it up by mistake when I was having a bubble bath. It ended up in the bin covered in trash. I was really upset. But then Henrietta bought me a new one. After that, I didn't look back. That's what you need," she added brightly. "A *new* lucky charm."

Coco smiled. It had turned out to be quite a speech. And everyone seemed to be listening, even though they couldn't all understand her.

Bernardo had been listening hardest of all. He had a strange look in his eye: a sort of twinkly glow, like a set

of Christmas-tree lights. Suddenly he jumped up, grabbed Coco's paw and started kissing it. "Señorita!" he cried. "That is a brilliant idea! And it has given me an even better one!" He let out a quick volley of Spanish.

The other guinea pigs crowded around Coco.

Bernardo reached for his guitar and began to play. "Come, everyone. Let's celebrate!"

The guinea pigs squeaked and chattered and danced. The two babies scampered to the table and returned with a piece of green tinsel. They shaped it into a circle and placed it on top of Coco's head, like a crown.

"What's happening?" Coco asked. "I'm confused."

"I have no idea," Fuzzy said, getting off his cushion, "but it looks like a lot of fun." He joined in the celebration.

Only Eduardo remained seated. "Now look what you've done," he said impatiently.

"What?" Coco said. "What have I done?"

"They think they have a new lucky charm," Eduardo growled, folding his front paws across his chest. "They think they don't need the lucky Christmas Cocoa Bean anymore. All because of *you*." He sounded furious.

"Me? But why?" Coco squeaked. "I don't understand!"

"Because you told them they could just get another one," Eduardo shouted over the din, "and your name is Coco. They think *you* are their new lucky charm!"

The procession came to a halt. The Queen of the Agoutis gave a nod.

Bernardo dropped down on his knees in front of Coco. "You are our guest of honor, Señorita Coco Loco del Posho of Buckingham Palace. We are at your service." He wiggled his whiskers. "Can I tempt you to a traditional Peruvian mud bath?" he suggested. "It really makes your fur shine."

"Pah!" Eduardo said in disgust. "I can't take no more of this. We must recover our lucky Christmas Cocoa Bean from the condor before it is too late. Or there won't be no more Christmases!"

He got up to fetch his satchel.

Coco stared after
him. She hadn't
wanted this to
happen. It wasn't
her fault. Anyway,
for all Eduardo
knew, she *could* be
the Agoutis' new
lucky charm. *Why
not?* She was better than
some moldy old cocoa bean any day.

She fluffed out her fur and gave
Bernardo a dazzling smile. "OK," she
said, "I'll have the mud bath. But can
I chew my chickweed while I soak?"

5
the giant bird

"Listen to me, *amigos*!" Eduardo cried out to all the guinea pigs in the burrow.

No one took any notice.

"OK, don't listen!" cried Eduardo.

And no one did listen. But he went ahead anyway.

"Remember . . . remember our great guinea-pig hero Indiana Pig!"

But no one did remember. They just carried on with what they were doing. And Eduardo carried on with his speech:

"Indiana Pig wasn't scared of the condor. It was he who built the plane and flew to the top of the mountain to fight the mighty bird. Now we must follow in his paw-steps. We must find the plane and fix it. Then we can fly up to the condor's nest and snatch our lucky Christmas Cocoa Bean back from under his beak. Who's with me? Who, who, who?"

"No one," Bernardo said. "You'd have to be crazy to do something like that."

Fuzzy hesitated. He wanted to help Eduardo, but his plan sounded impossible. "Coco," he whispered, "what should we do?"

"I can recommend the mud bath," Coco replied, lying back and relaxing.

"Pah! Then I will do it alone!"

Eduardo turned and marched out of the burrow. He looked up toward the top of the mountain. The snow-capped peaks glistened. The plane

condor's nest. He took a deep breath. If Indiana Pig wasn't scared of the condor, then neither was he.

He opened up his satchel and rummaged for his ski poles. Then he realized he'd left them in the burrow. All he had were some cotton swabs that he'd found in the thicket. "Holy guacamole!" he muttered to himself. "This is going to take a while." He held one in each paw and stuck the bottom ends into the snow. Luckily no one had used them to clean their ears yet, so there wasn't any yucky earwax on the ends. He trudged forward, poking the sticks into the snow every time he took a step.

Eduardo plodded up the mountain, paw by paw. It started to snow and he had to put his head down to keep the snowflakes out of his eyes. He thought of nice things to keep him going. He thought of his friend Fuzzy and the way he danced on computer keyboards to write messages. He thought of his friend Coco and the pretty little bow in her hair. He thought of Indiana Pig and his brave adventure in the plane. He thought

about how happy his mother would be
when he brought back the cocoa bean
from the condor's nest.

After he had thought of all these
things he stopped for a moment and

rested. And, very quickly, he nodded off.

"QUARK!"

Eduardo opened an eye. What was that terrible noise?

"QUARK!"

There it was again. He opened the other eye. Something was tickling his nose. It felt like a giant feather. He looked down. It *was* a giant feather. And it was attached to a giant bird.

The condor!

"What's the problem, buddy?" said a loud, deep voice from above

his head. Eduardo looked up. A
huge glassy eye was staring at him.
Eduardo was terrified! He looked
all around, searching for a way to
escape. But there was none. He was
surrounded by black feathers. Just
then the feathers lifted, and Eduardo
saw that he was at the very top of
the mountain, on a pile of twigs.
The condor had taken him to his
nest!

"Let me go!" Eduardo shouted.

"You ain't going nowhere," said
the voice. "No one escapes the mighty
Peruvian condor."

"You don't sound very Peruvian," said Eduardo.

"I stole a laptop from some tourists. I watch a lot of films on it: American mainly. I picked up the accent."

The condor flicked Eduardo with his enormous black wing, pushing him back onto something hard. Eduardo turned around to see what he had landed on. He couldn't believe his eyes—the Lucky Christmas Cocoa Bean!

The condor laughed. "You pleased to see your little buddy again? Well, don't go thinking you're walking off into the sunset together. You're both finished."

The condor fished under the twigs and emerged with his laptop. He balanced it on the nest and tapped the keyboard with a claw.

"So, tell me the names of your buddies down the mountain. Maybe they'd like to join you."

"I'm not telling you nothing!"
Eduardo shouted.

The condor shrugged. He pinned
Eduardo down with one claw and
tapped away on the keyboard with
the other. "I know their names
anyway. I found them on Micespace.
Coco, ain't it? And Fuzzy?"

Eduardo struggled, but
he couldn't get free.

"Got a message
for them?" asked
the condor. "Apart
from HELP!"

6
mountain mission

"What's this?"

Fuzzy and Coco were back in the cabin playing on Mummy's phone with the Agoutis when a message came through on Micespace.

The guinea pigs crowded round.

Buenas tardes, amigos! It is I, Eduardo.

"That's odd," Fuzzy frowned. "I didn't know Eduardo had a cellphone."

"He doesn't," Coco said. She tried to sit down beside Fuzzy but slipped over because her fur was so silky from the mud bath. "Only ski poles."

"And he doesn't know how to get onto Micespace without me." Fuzzy scratched his crest. "If I didn't know better, I'd say this was Renard up to his old tricks."

"Renard?" Coco said. "But he's in the thicket, back in England."

"Hmm," Fuzzy said. "Maybe

he's tipped off a pal. We'd better be careful."

Where are you? he typed.

Hanging out at the top of the mountain with a friend, came the reply.

Bernardo snorted. "It's definitely not Eduardo," he said unkindly. "He doesn't have any friends."

Coco glared at him. "Yes, he does," she snapped. "He's got me and Fuzzy."

"That's right," Fuzzy agreed.

Sounds fun, he typed. He winked at Coco. **What's your friend's name?**

There was a pause.

Dronco.

"Dronco?" Coco exclaimed. "That's a funny name for a guinea pig."

"It's a funny name for anyone," Fuzzy said thoughtfully. He grabbed a bit of paper and a pencil. Quickly he scribbled down the letters that made up the name Dronco:

O . . . D . . . C . . . N . . . O . . . R.

"Why have you muddled them up?" Coco asked, puzzled.

"So that I can see if they make another word," Fuzzy explained. "It's called an anagram. They use them in crosswords. I want to find out who it is we're really talking to. I've got a bad feeling it isn't Eduardo."

Coco stared at the letters. It was true. When you mixed them up you could make different words out of them.

"Codron?" she suggested.

"Nodroc?" Bernardo tried to help.

Fuzzy shook his head. He looked grim. He circled each letter one by one with the pencil:

C . . . O . . . N . . . D . . . O . . . R.

"The condor!" Bernardo whispered.

"Oh no!" Coco gulped. "The condor's got Eduardo."

All the guinea pigs started squeaking. They knew what the word condor meant. It was the same in Spanish and English.

"We'll pretend we don't know it's really him," Fuzzy said. "See what he wants." **Dronco sounds cool!** he typed.

Yeah, he's great! He's going to help me get the cocoa bean. And he's organizing a Christmas feast at the top of the mountain. He wants you all to come.

Coco and Fuzzy glanced at one another. "I bet he does!" Coco muttered.

Sure! Fuzzy typed back. **We'll be there.** He switched off the phone.

"Are you crazy?" Bernardo said. "The only thing on the menu at the condor's Christmas feast will be guinea pig."

"I know," Fuzzy said. "But we have to help Eduardo."

"Of course we do!" Coco agreed. "He's rescued me twice from the fox. Now it's our turn to rescue him from the condor."

"Count me out!" Bernardo said. "I'm not going anywhere."

"But he's your cousin!" Coco insisted. "And it's Christmas! You can't just do nothing. And anyway, we don't know the way. You've got to help us!"

"There's only one guinea pig who knows the way to the condor's nest, since Indiana Pig disappeared," Bernardo sighed.

"Who is it?" Coco asked.

"Sherpa Shorty," Bernardo said. "He was Indiana Pig's guide."

"You mean he's still alive?" Coco demanded.

"That depends on what mood he's in," Bernardo said. "Come, I will take you to him."

"If only he could find the plane!"

Fuzzy muttered. "Then we could fly up there and rescue Eduardo."

Sherpa Shorty lived beside a stream in a little house made of twigs.

KNOCK. KNOCK. KNOCK.
Coco and Fuzzy hammered at the door with Bernardo.

"Go away," a sleepy voice squeaked. "I'm hibernating."

"No, you're not!" Bernardo said. "Guinea pigs don't hibernate."

"I'm dead then."

"If you're dead, how come you're talking?" Fuzzy inquired.

"Oh, all right!" the voice grumbled. "I'm coming."

They heard shuffling. Then the door opened.

"Where is he?" Coco whispered, peering in.

"Down here!" the voice answered impatiently.

The guinea pigs looked down. A very short guinea pig with tufty gray fur stood in front of them. He wore a red-and-white striped hat pulled down over his ears. "What do you want?"

"We need to go to the condor's nest," Coco explained.

"To rescue our friend Eduardo," Fuzzy said.

"He's my cousin. He's being held captive," Bernardo added.

"Can't help you." 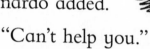 Sherpa Shorty tried to close the door.

"Please!" Coco wedged the door open with her paw. "He went to rescue the lucky Christmas Cocoa Bean. The condor guinea-pig-napped him. You've got to help us! You're our only hope! He was following in the paw-steps of Indiana Pig!"

Sherpa Shorty started. "Indiana Pig?" he said. "I remember him."

"Do you know the way?" Fuzzy asked eagerly.

"Well . . ." Sherpa Shorty hesitated. "Sort of."

"That's good enough." Coco grabbed his whiskers and started to drag him out. "Come on."

"Wait!" Sherpa Shorty pulled free and scuttled back into the twig house. He opened a cupboard and began chucking things out onto the floor. "We'll need some equipment," he grunted.

Fuzzy and Coco watched
as one item after another whizzed
through the air and onto the pile.

"Elastic bands . . ." Sherpa Shorty
muttered.

"Rope . . .

"Toilet paper . . .

"Soap . . .

"Toothpaste . . .

"More rope . . ."

"Hurry up!" Coco grumbled. "We
haven't got all day."

Sherpa Shorty filled up a guinea-
pig-size backpack and slung it on his
back.

They waved good-bye to Bernardo and set off through the snow.

"Er . . . shouldn't we be going uphill?" Fuzzy asked.

"I knew that," Sherpa Shorty said impatiently. He turned around and set off the other way. They said good-bye to Bernardo again.

After a little while Sherpa Shorty stopped. "We'll pitch camp here," he announced.

"What are you talking about?" Coco said. "We only left five minutes ago. We'll never get there at this rate."

"He's asleep," Fuzzy said.

Sherpa Shorty lay in the snow under the backpack, snoring loudly.

"You take this," Fuzzy said, peeling the backpack off Sherpa Shorty and giving it to Coco. "I'll take him." He hoisted Sherpa Shorty onto his back.

"This is hopeless!" Coco moaned. The backpack kept sliding off her silky fur. And it was very, very heavy.

"I bet the Queen never has to do anything like this. I wish we

could bump into Rupert de Vere," she sighed. "He'd be bound to help us."

Just at that moment Coco *did* bump into something. She stared hard at it. It wasn't Rupert de Vere, she decided, unless he had very hairy legs. Four of them.

"Husky!" Fuzzy shouted. "Boy, are we pleased to see you!"

7
the nestbusters

"What are you guys doing out in the snow?" said Husky.

"We're going up the mountain to rescue Eduardo," Coco told him.

"He went to get the lucky Christmas Cocoa Bean back from the condor," Fuzzy said. He started to explain what had happened. When he got to the bit about Indiana Pig and the plane he was interrupted by a snorting noise.

"Your backpack seems to be snoring," Husky said.

"It's not a backpack, it's our mountain guide." Fuzzy let Sherpa Shorty slide gently to the ground.

Sherpa Shorty opened his eyes, lifted his head, and pointed up the mountain.

"You need to go that way," he said, and then fell back asleep.

Husky lowered his head and gently

flicked Sherpa Shorty onto his back.
"We'd better take him with us. We
might need some more directions
when we get to the top of the
mountain."

"You mean, *you're* coming with
us?" said Coco excitedly. "But what

about the humans? Don't they need your help to find the gold?"

"Mummy can track me if she needs me."

"How can she do that?" asked Fuzzy.

"With this!" Husky pointed at his collar with his back paw. "It's got all

the latest gadgets. You know what Mummy's like."

The little party set off up the mountain.

As they neared the summit, the slope became rockier and steeper, until Husky was forced to stop at a sheer cliff face.

"That's too steep for me," said Husky.

"If only we could find the plane," Fuzzy said despairingly.

Husky stared out at the snow. He lifted his head and wiggled his wet, black nose.

"Hang on," he said. "I can smell something . . ."

He sniffed. "It's engine oil . . ."

He took a few steps forward and turned his head to one side.

"It's this way!" He trotted off into the snow. "Follow me!" After a minute, he stopped. "Here!" Husky dumped

Sherpa Shorty on the snow and started to dig with his front paws.

"The plane!" Coco gasped.

The red cockpit of Indiana Pig's long-lost plane began to emerge from the snow.

Husky lifted it out gently with his teeth.

"Is it damaged?" Coco asked.

"There's only one way to find

out!" Fuzzy cried. He jumped into the pilot's seat. Coco climbed in behind him.

"Wait for me!" Sherpa Shorty flung the backpack in after them and leaped in beside Fuzzy.

Coco glared at him. "I thought you were asleep!" she shouted.

"I only sleep when there's something I don't want to do—" Sherpa Shorty grinned "—like carrying a heavy backpack!"

Fuzzy pressed the starter button. He pushed down on one of the pedals with his foot. They all held their

breath as the engine made a strange
growling noise.

"That doesn't sound good!" said
Coco.

She felt very afraid, but Eduardo
was in terrible danger. They had to
rescue him! Eduardo had rescued her
in the past, and now it was their turn
to save him. The plane was their only
chance.

Fuzzy flicked the button again. He pushed his foot down harder on the pedal.

After a long growl, the engine finally came to life.

HMMMMMMMMMMMMM! The plane purred.

"Hurray!" said Coco. "It's working!"

"Fasten your seat belts!" Fuzzy shouted. "Hold tight, ready for takeoff."

"Good luck!" Husky barked.

Fuzzy carefully drove the plane across the snow and onto a flat piece

of land. He revved the engine again
and accelerated. The front of the
plane lifted into the air and began to
climb. Then, when the ground was far
beneath them, he leveled the plane out
and gently turned it around.

"Wow!" cried Coco. "We're up so
high!"

Husky waved from below.

"Husky's shrinking!" cried Sherpa Shorty, full of alarm.

"No, he's not," explained Coco. "We're going higher so he *looks* smaller."

"But what if he disappears like Indiana Pig?" said Sherpa.

"Don't look down," suggested Coco.

Sherpa looked up instead. "Now the clouds are getting bigger!" he yelled.

"Just shut your eyes," said Coco impatiently.

Sherpa shut his eyes and immediately fell asleep.

Fuzzy turned the plane upward and slightly to the left. They were heading toward the mountain peak where the condor lived.

Coco leaned forward and patted him on the shoulder. "Well done, Fuzzy," she said.

Fuzzy smiled proudly. It was nice to be good at something, especially something as exciting as flying a plane. And Coco didn't often say nice things. So when she did, you knew she meant them.

"There's the nest!" said Coco.

The guinea pigs could see the

condor's vast flapping wings, but there was no sign of Eduardo. Fuzzy gulped. Perhaps they were too late!

"Coming in to land!" he shouted. "Hold on."

The plane's nose tipped down. The engine whirred. There was a roar, then a bump, then a screech of brakes. The plane came to a juddering halt on the packed snow next to the nest.

"Eduardo!" Coco leaped out. She could see a small pair of silvery black paws sticking out from a laptop—the condor had trapped Eduardo between

the keyboard and the lid! Coco rushed
toward it.

"*QUARK!* Bang on time! I'm
hungry!" a voice croaked.

Coco looked up in horror. A big
glassy eye stared back at her.

"Coco! Watch out!" Fuzzy tore

open the backpack and looked inside.
There must be something in there
he could use against the condor.
He searched frantically. There
was nothing but toothpaste and—
TOOTHPASTE! Fuzzy remembered
how Ben squeezed the tube and the
paste squeezed onto his toothbrush.
Maybe he could do the same.

"Sherpa Shorty!" he squeaked.
"Help me!"

Sherpa Shorty woke up with a
start. He got out of the plane and
scurried over to help.

"Squeeze the end!" Fuzzy yelled.

Sherpa Shorty pressed on the tube with all his might, while Fuzzy held it up toward the condor.

SPLAT!

"Take that, loser!" Fuzzy shouted.

A huge blob of toothpaste landed in the condor's eye. He yelped in alarm.

Another big splotch
landed in his other
eye. He couldn't
see! The bird
staggered
backward,
trying to wipe the
toothpaste away with
its wing.

SPLAT! SQUISH!
SPLAT!

Sherpa Shorty
jumped up and down
on the tube.

Coco flung herself at the laptop

lid and managed to force it open. Eduardo rolled off the keyboard.

"About time!" he complained, straightening his whiskers.

"Any minute now the toothpaste will run out!" Fuzzy shouted. He chucked the backpack toward his friends.

Coco and Eduardo scampered over to it and scrabbled inside for another weapon.

"Hey, beak-face, your wing-pits smell. Why don't you take a bath!" Eduardo flung the soap under the condor's feet.

The enormous bird slipped on it and stumbled. *"QUARK!"* it squawked angrily.

"Time to play!" Eduardo grabbed some of the rope from the backpack. He crept behind the condor and lassoed its leg.

"Pull!"

He and Coco heaved on the other end of the rope.

The condor finally fell over. Eduardo laughed. "Not so tough now!" he said as he tied the condor's feet together.

Fuzzy raced over. He scooped up

the toilet roll and wound it around and around the condor's beak. "That should hold him for a while!"

"We need to take the cocoa bean down the mountain," Eduardo shouted.

"You've found it!" Coco cried. She felt like hugging him but it didn't seem the right time.

"*Si*, señorita. It was hidden in the

nest. Come on!" Eduardo grabbed the cocoa bean, threw it in his satchel, and ran toward the plane.

The guinea pigs scurried after him. They all hopped into the plane. There was just enough room for all of them. Fuzzy revved the engine and took off into the sky.

8
flight

"Wow! You can fly a plane, *amigo*!"
Eduardo clapped Fuzzy on the back
with his paw.

"It's thanks to all those adventure
films I watch with Ben," Fuzzy explained.

"That is not only clever but also
amazing!" Eduardo yelled.

Just then the plane started to jolt.

"The condor!" shouted Fuzzy. "He's escaped!"

"I told you he had a beak like a pair of *skissors*!" Eduardo yelled. "He must have used it to cut through the rope!"

"And the toilet roll!" Fuzzy cried.

"You betcha!" The condor lunged at them with his giant wings.

Fuzzy tried to keep the plane level, but when the condor gave it one last shove it tipped down toward the ground. Fuzzy clung onto the stick.

"We're going to crash!" squeaked Coco, alarmed.

"Mayday! Mayday!" shouted Fuzzy. "The plane's out of control!"

"Well, get it in control!" Coco shrieked. "Surely those films taught you how to do that."

"In the films the planes didn't get shoved by a condor!" Fuzzy yelled back.

Coco looked shocked. "Help!" she squealed. The ground loomed toward them.

"The soft Peruvian snow will help us!" cried Eduardo.

"Hold on!" Fuzzy yelled.

The guinea pigs braced themselves. *BOOMPH!*

There was a crash. The guinea pigs were thrown forward and then backward.

The plane juddered to a halt.

"Is everyone OK?" Fuzzy glanced round.

The others nodded. They were too shaken to say anything. Silently they wriggled out. Eduardo pulled Sherpa Shorty clear.

"That's that, then." Fuzzy looked at the plane sadly. The wings had broken off. It would never fly again.

"What do we do now?" Coco whispered.

"Quick!" Eduardo shouted. The condor was still circling above them. "Get your skis."

"What skis?" Coco yelped.

"These!" Eduardo grabbed a propeller blade and swung on it until it snapped off. He reached up, grabbed another blade and snapped that one off too. "For you, señorita." He chucked them on the ground beside Coco.

Eduardo gave Coco two more cotton buds from his satchel. Then Coco grabbed a bit of rope from the backpack and used it to tie her right foot to the propeller blade. She did the same with her left foot.

"What an excellent idea, señorita!" said Eduardo. "I shall do the same!"

He snapped off two more blades and fixed them onto his feet.

"I've always fancied snowboarding myself!" Fuzzy grabbed one of the broken wings to make a snowboard. He gave the other one to Sherpa Shorty.

WHOOSH!

"Follow me!" Eduardo called out to the others as he set off down the mountain.

"It's all right for you," Coco shouted after him. "You grew up on the snow.

It hardly ever snows in Strawberry Park, except on the television."

Eduardo didn't answer because he couldn't hear her. He was already a long way down the mountain.

"WHEEEE!" Fuzzy quickly got the hang of snowboarding. He raced after Eduardo.

Sherpa Shorty wasn't far behind.

"Come on, Coco," Fuzzy shouted. "It's easy!"

"OK, here goes." She dug her ski poles into the snow and pushed forward. She moved off down the mountain. She felt pleased she'd figured out how to start skiing. *But what about stopping?* She didn't know how to do that!

"Heeeellllllpppppp!" she squealed as she bumped over the snow.

CRASH!

She slammed into the back of Sherpa Shorty.

BASH!

Sherpa Shorty went tumbling into Fuzzy.

SMASH!

Fuzzy crashed into Eduardo.

The guinea pigs lay on the ground in a tangled heap.

"Is everyone OK?" Fuzzy glanced around again.

The shadow of the condor loomed over them. He was back!

"Now what?" Fuzzy panted.

Just then they heard barking.

"Husky!" Coco cried.

The guinea pigs watched as Husky

leaped at the condor and barked.

"Is that the best you've got?" The condor swooped and dived at Husky's ears.

"We need to find shelter," Husky shouted. "I can't hold him off for long."

The guinea pigs scuttled toward the overhanging rock. Husky charged after them, panting.

"We should hide in the secret cave," Sherpa Shorty announced. "Like I did with Indiana Pig."

"But we don't know where it is," Fuzzy said.

"There's a secret door," Sherpa Shorty said.

"How do you know?" Coco said rudely. "You can't remember anything."

"I can now, since you bumped into me," Sherpa Shorty said. "You jogged my memory." He peered at the rock face closely. "It's definitely around here somewhere."

The others waited impatiently.

The condor circled, getting ready for another attack.

"Hurry, *amigo*!" Eduardo said nervously. "Or we will become the condor's Christmas dinner after all."

"Here!" Sherpa Shorty pointed to a carving of a human face on the rock.

Husky stared at it. "This is it!" he whispered. "The entrance to Magchu Pigchu! This is what the humans have been looking for! This is the way to the lost Inca gold."

He pressed the carving with his paw.

The mountain gave a shudder. To the guinea pigs' amazement, the rock began to part. A huge crack, just wide enough for a human to squeeze through, appeared as a section of rock slid to one side.

The animals raced in.

"Quick!" Eduardo shouted. "Close it! The condor is coming."

The bird's shadow was getting bigger.

Husky's paw pressed a second carving inside the passageway.

Slowly the rock face started to close.

CLUNK!

The secret door slid back into place.

SPLAT! The condor flew into the rock. They were safe!

"I'll be back!" the bird shrieked.

"Phew!" Eduardo breathed a sigh of relief. "Well done, *amigos*. I'm glad to see the back of him!" He looked around. "Now we need to find another way out."

9
the lost gold

"Are you sure this is the place Mummy and Dolores are looking for?" Coco asked Husky. She reached out and found Fuzzy's paw. It was scary in the dark.

"Yes," Husky said. "The carving on the rock face is definitely an Inca carving. This must be the place." He lifted a back paw and flicked at his collar. The studs on it flashed green, red, and blue.

"What are you doing?" Fuzzy asked.

"I've turned my tracker device on so that Mummy can find us."

"That's cool," Fuzzy said. "Does your collar do anything else?"

Husky's eyes twinkled. "Maybe," he said. He padded away from the door in the rock toward the center of the mountain. "Follow me."

The guinea pigs scampered after Husky into the secret passageway. It was pitch black except for Husky's collar, which glowed in the dark. After a few minutes, Husky stopped abruptly.

"We found it!" he whispered.

The guinea pigs stared. They were standing at the entrance of a huge cave. They peered in. The cave was piled high

with heaps of gold. It twinkled in the dim light of Husky's collar.

"Holy guacamole!" Eduardo said. "No one said nothing about this!"

"Indiana Pig told me to keep it secret." Sherpa Shorty scratched his hat. "He didn't want any of the other guinea pigs to know about it. He was worried about disturbing the ghosts of the Incas. Anyway," he added, "I'd forgotten about it until just now."

Coco started forward toward a stack of bracelets. "I'm just having a look!" she said. Husky looked as if he might tell her off.

Just then they heard a noise. It sounded like a human talking.

"Is that Mummy?" Fuzzy asked doubtfully.

Husky pricked up his ears. "Not unless she's turned into a man," he said.

"One's found it," a grand voice said. "At last! Bring the bags. We'll take what we can now and come back for the rest later."

"It's the robbers!" Eduardo hissed. "What shall we do?"

"Over here." Husky led the way silently behind a pile of gold coins.

The guinea pigs followed him. Except Coco, who was too busy checking out the bracelets to notice anything was wrong.

The voice became louder. "Jolly good show, gentlemen," it said. "One didn't expect it to be as easy as this!" The owner of the grand voice bent down and started to scoop handfuls of gold into his pockets.

"Look at these beauties!" The robber snatched up a

handful of gold coins. He frowned as he felt something furry.

It was Coco. She stared at the robber in horror—Rupert de Vere!

"Why is there a guinea pig in my treasure?" Rupert de Vere demanded. He dangled Coco in front of him. "Wait a minute. You're the one from the plane!"

"Woof!"

Rupert de Vere looked round wildly. "A dog as well? What is this—a zoo?"

ZIP!

Coco saw a thin rope whizz through the air and attach itself to the cave ceiling above Rupert de Vere's head.

There was a shout. Suddenly a blur of black and silver shot through the air on the other end of the rope.

"Eduardo!" Coco cried. She leaped out of Rupert de Vere's hand and grabbed onto Eduardo's tummy as he hurtled past.

Rupert de Vere was too surprised to stop her.

"At your service, señorita," Eduardo grinned.

They landed in a heap on the cave floor. "How did you do that?" Coco gasped.

"Señor Husky fired the rope from his collar," Eduardo explained. "All I had to do was swing on it." His eyes twinkled. "Man, what I could do with a gadget like that."

"Woof!"

PING!

"Now what's happening?" Rupert de Vere said in astonishment. "Ouch!" A gold coin hit him in the eye.

Another one hit him on the nose.

The other members of Rupert De Vere's gang looked around nervously.

Coco and Eduardo scuttled across the floor to where Fuzzy and Sherpa Shorty were pinging gold coins at the robbers with the elastic bands from the backpack.

"Aim!" Husky woofed. "Fire!"

"Ouch!"

"It's the ghosts of the Incas!" one of the gang said. "I'm out of here."

"Me too," agreed another one.

Before long they had all disappeared.

"You cowards!" Rupert de Vere

shouted after them. "Oh well, now the treasure is all mine!"

"No, it isn't!" Coco muttered. Rupert de Vere was a crook. His pretend good manners were getting up her nose. Suddenly she had an idea. It wasn't very ladylike, but it was an emergency, after all. "Can you give us some more rope, Husky?"

ZIP!

Husky fired another line from his collar into the cave ceiling.

Coco rummaged in Eduardo's satchel. "These will do." She pulled out the cotton-bud ski poles. Then she lifted up Sherpa Shorty's hat and stuffed the cotton swabs into his ears.

"What do you think you're doing?" he cried.

"Sorry about that," Coco said, "but it is an emergency. And your ears needed a good cleaning anyway."

Holding the clean ends of the cotton swabs in her mouth, she scrambled up the pile of gold coins.

Eduardo wiggled his eyebrows. "Would you like some help, señorita?" he said.

"Yes, one would," she grinned.

Husky picked Eduardo up gently

in his mouth and flipped him onto the gold-coin mountain next to Coco. Coco handed Eduardo a cotton swab.

"Woof!" Husky shot another rope into the ceiling.

The guinea pigs caught hold of a rope each with their free paws. They launched themselves into the air.

WHOOSH!

Coco and Eduardo flew toward Rupert de Vere.

He stared at them in astonishment. "What the . . . ?"

"Hold steady, Eduardo!" Coco shouted. She gripped her cotton swab

in one paw. "Wait till
I give the signal."

"OK, señorita!"
Eduardo gripped
his cotton swab.

The guinea
pigs hurtled toward
Rupert de Vere's
face. He took a
step back.

"Now!" Coco shoved a waxy
cotton swab up his right nostril.

"Take that!" Eduardo shoved a
waxy cotton swab up his left nostril.

"Aaarrrrggghhh!"

Rupert de Vere
screamed.

It wasn't
surprising really.
Most people would
scream if two
guinea pigs shoved
cotton swabs covered
in earwax up
their nostrils.

Then he fell over, because Husky
had bitten him on the ankle.

Coco and Eduardo dropped from
the ropes onto Husky's back.

Fuzzy and Sherpa Shorty rushed

over to join them.

Just then Mummy, Henrietta, Ben, and Dolores arrived at the mouth of the cave from the other direction.

"It's the gold!" Dolores cried.

"It's the robber!" Ben cried.

"It's Rupert de Vere!" Mummy shouted. "The beast!"

"Why has he got two dirty cotton swabs shoved up his nose?" Henrietta gave a little shudder.

Then they saw Husky and the guinea pigs.

"What are *you* doing here,

Fuzzy?" Ben picked him up.

"What are *you* doing here, Coco?" Henrietta picked her up.

"What are *they* doing here?" Dolores picked up Eduardo and Sherpa Shorty, which they both liked because they didn't have human owners and didn't get many cuddles.

"Good job, Husky!" Mummy said. "I knew that collar would come in handy. Now let's phone the museum and tell them we've found the gold!"

10
a snowy christmas

"Happy Christmas, Henrietta!" said Mummy.

"Happy Christmas, Mummy," said Henrietta. "Who'd have thought we'd be spending it in Peru!"

"I'm sorry to have taken you away from Christmas at home," said Dolores.

"Don't be sorry," said Ben. "We've had a big adventure, we've rescued the Inca gold and we're even having a traditional Christmas dinner!"

Everyone watched as Henrietta carved the turkey and Ben passed around the roast potatoes. Dolores had even organized crackers on the table, complete with hats, gifts, and silly jokes.

"One sprout or two?" Ben asked Fuzzy as he placed the steaming

vegetables on a little saucer at the end of the table where Coco, Fuzzy and Husky were sitting.

"Three," Fuzzy replied. Ben didn't understand guinea-pig squeaks, but gave Fuzzy four Brussels sprouts because it was Christmas. Coco also had four Brussels sprouts and Husky had a huge bowl of turkey and gravy. There was a happy silence as everyone enjoyed their Christmas dinner.

"Isn't this amazing?" said Fuzzy after his third Brussels sprout. He needed a little break before he took on the fourth. "We're having exactly the same Christmas as we would have had in Strawberry Park."

"It's not *exactly* the same," said Coco, a bit sadly, "because we haven't got any presents."

"Coco!" exclaimed Fuzzy. "How can you be so greedy? After what happened with the condor we're lucky to be alive. Isn't that enough?"

"Of course it is," replied Coco, "but I thought the humans might just give us a couple of little things, to thank us for everything we did for them."

"Yes, but they don't know what we did," said Husky wisely.

"True," said Coco, and went back to nibbling her fourth Brussels sprout.

When everyone had finished, Dolores clapped her hands. "Time for presents!" she announced.

"Presents?" said Henrietta, surprised. "But we left them in London."

"The museum has given us some presents," Mummy said. "As a thank-you for finding the gold." She got up from the table, went over to her old handbag, and pulled out a pile of Christmas presents, complete with name tags and a few toffees. Dolores handed out the presents. There was one for everyone, including the animals!

Inside Coco's parcel was a brand-new gold-colored bow.

Fuzzy had a gold-colored comb for his crest and Husky had a gold-colored collar. The animals were all thrilled.

"Happy?" Fuzzy whispered.

"So happy!" Coco whispered back.

After opening the presents, the humans dozed off.

"Let's go and see Eduardo," Fuzzy suggested.

He and Coco slipped down the tunnel under the stove.

In the burrow, Eduardo's brothers and sisters were happily playing with their new toys. Sherpa Shorty was snoozing by the fire. Bernardo sat opposite him, strumming on his guitar. Eduardo was polishing his skis.

As soon as everyone saw Fuzzy and Coco, they stopped what they were doing and greeted their friends.

"You are just in time for the Queen's speech," said Eduardo.

"Oh good," said Coco. "One always used to play the harp for Her Majesty while she wrote it."

"I don't mean the British Queen," Eduardo said. "I mean the Queen of the Agoutis."

Just then Eduardo's mom came out of the kitchen wearing her crown. She sat at the head of the table and took a sip of papaya juice. Eduardo translated her wise words so Coco and Fuzzy could understand what she was saying.

"*Amigos, niños,* friends and family. It is my pleasure to welcome you all.

"I have seen many Christmases here in the burrow and they have all been happy," the Queen continued, "but this is the happiest Christmas of all. Not only do I have all my family around me, I have dear friends from London." She paused. "And, thanks to them and to Eduardo, I have, once again, the lucky Christmas Cocoa Bean, restored to its home, here on our table."

She gestured to the cocoa bean, which sat in the middle of the table on the green tinsel.

The guinea pigs clapped.

"With the cocoa bean restored we will be safe from the condor and other dangers for the year to come."

The guinea pigs cheered.

"So let us give thanks—to the brave guinea pigs who climbed the mountain, in the footsteps of the great Indiana Pig, to bring back the lucky Christmas Bean."

Everyone turned to Eduardo, Fuzzy, and Coco, who were sitting together. Eduardo and Fuzzy put their paws around Coco, and Coco put her paws around them. Everyone cheered louder than ever.

Coco felt a funny feeling in her stomach. It couldn't be hunger: she'd eaten five whole Brussels sprouts (she'd pinched the one Fuzzy had left on his saucer). The feeling went right through her body and out through her eyes, which sparkled. Although she was thousands of miles from home she felt loved and loving, and that, she decided, was the best Christmas present of all.

the end

Be Safe Online!

Surfing the internet is lots of fun, but there are some things Coco and Fuzzy want you to remember so that you stay safe online . . .

GUINEA PIGS ONLINE

G is for *Go Away!*
Never chat online with people you don't know. Never reply to messages from people you don't know. Finally, never, ever agree to meet up with someone you have only met online—it could be dangerous!

P is for *Private!*
Never tell anyone your personal information, like where you live, your phone number, or your passwords. It's your private information and that's how it should stay—private.

O is for *Oh Really?*
You really can't trust everything you read on the internet. Check any information you learn online with an adult to make sure it's true—you might be surprised how much false information is out there!

L is for *Let an Adult Know*
Finally, you should always let an adult know about what you're doing on the internet. And if you're worried about something that you've seen or read online, tell a grown-up right away—adults can be really good at explaining things that might seem mysterious to you.

You're much better at using
the Internet than Coco is . . .

. . . so why not visit

www.guinea-pigs-online.com

for lots more fun, giggles and squeaks
with your favorite furry pals!

about the authors and illustrator

Jennifer Gray is a lawyer. She lives in central London and Scotland with her husband, four children, and an overfed cat, Henry. Jennifer's other books for children include a comedy series about Atticus Claw, the world's greatest cat burglar.

Amanda Swift has written for several well-established children's TV series, including *My Parents Are Aliens*; she has also written three novels for middle-grade readers: *The Boys' Club, Big Bones,* and *Anna/Bella*. She lives in southeast London, near the Olympic park. Unlike Coco, she hasn't met the queen.

Sarah Horne was born in Stockport, Cheshire, on a snowy November day, and grew up scampering in the fields surrounding Buxton, Derbyshire. She is propelled by a generous dose of slapstick, a love for color and line, a clever story, and a good cup of coffee.